. . . and he won't be allowed to drive the fire engine till he's got Experience.

In Basic Training, firefighters learn how to use all sorts of Special Equipment. They learn that fire extinguishers must never be pointed at other people . . .

. . . and that the hose often has a Mind Of Its Own.

Firefighters also learn to use Common Sense. Common Sense is useful when you're rescuing people.

I'm upside down, Moose!

Apparently the safety net is for catching people, not for bouncing on.

After training, each firefighter joins a team called a Watch. This is Blue Watch. They're going to work the Night Shift.

Moose joins Red Watch. They will work the Day Shift.

They are all obviously Very Brave
– and they are all Ready for Anything.

They have 24 boots between them.

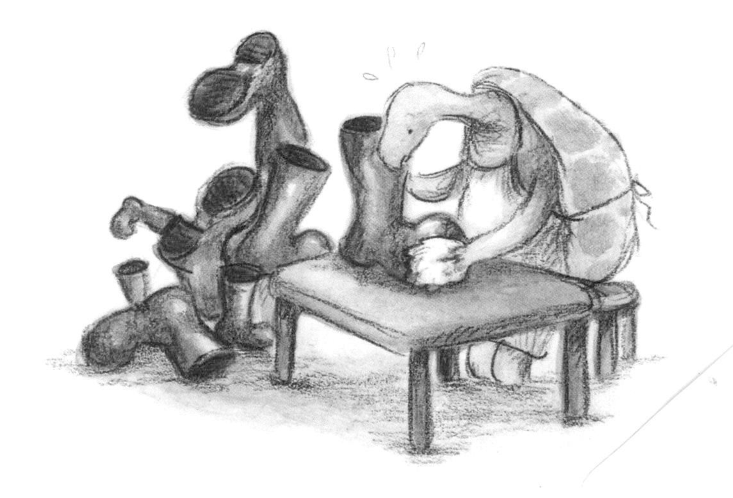

'EMERGENCY RESCUE!'

Firefighter Owl sits in the Control Room. She tells them when a Shout has come in. That means they have to rush off and rescue someone.

Sliding down a pole is quicker than running downstairs, especially when you're asleep.

Moose learns to get ready in Double-Quick Time.

Personal Protective Equipment is very heavy.

In just two minutes, the firefighters are ready to go.
Moose still isn't allowed to drive the fire engine . . .

. . . so he just shouts "Nee-naw! Nee-naw! Nee-naw!" as they drive along. This isn't strictly necessary, but it's fun.

Firefighters don't just tackle fires.

Here, a bushbaby has got stuck on a tall giraffe.

This ostrich is
trapped in a drain.

Dachshunds sometimes
get stuck up drainpipes.

And they often have to
pull a pig out of a pothole.

Back at the firestation, the firefighters can relax for a while in the Mess Room.

Moose is pretty handy at snooker.

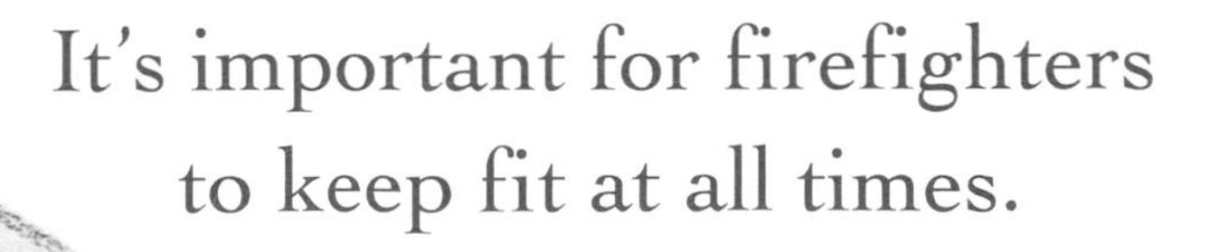

It's important for firefighters
to keep fit at all times.

Firefighters take turns to do the cooking. Today it's Firefighter Dog's turn.
He tends to just open a tin of something.

No one's very keen on Dog's dinner.

'EMERGENCY!
32 WARREN LANE!'

Luckily there isn't time to eat it.
The alarm goes, and it's Action Stations.
They're off to the rescue again!

For this rescue, the firefighters need their Breathing Apparatus.

Swoon!

Some skunks have let off a really stinky smell next to some rabbits.

The rabbits have fainted – but they will be fine after hospital treatment.

So will Firefighter Koala, who wasn't quite quick enough with his gas mask.

The rabbits are packed safely off to Hospital, but there's no time to relax. Another Shout has come in . . .

. . . and this time
it's an Actual Fire!

Station Officer Puffin quickly sizes up the situation.

It was Grandpa Tortoise's 249th birthday.

That's a lot of candles to have on a cake . . .

. . . and they set fire to the decorations!

The firefighters quickly rescue the tortoise family . . . but what about the twenty-one guinea-pigs on the top floor? They're too scared to jump, and it'll take ages to rescue them one by one!

Then Moose has a Bright Idea . . .

While the rest of the
Watch tackle the fire,
Moose bravely climbs
the ladder . . .

. . . and persuades every
single guinea-pig to climb
on to his antlers!

What a hero!

Everyone agrees that Moose has demonstrated Bravery and Quick Thinking.

Station Officer Puffin
awards him a medal.

And at long last . . .

RESCUE
FIRE
999

. . . he's allowed to drive the fire engine!
Congratulations, Firefighter Moose! Excellent work!

For Firefighter Peter and
also all the Firefighters at
Euston Fire Station.

First published in 2012 by Alison Green Books
An imprint of Scholastic Children's Books
Euston House, 24 Eversholt Street
London NW1 1DB
A division of Scholastic Ltd
www.scholastic.co.uk
London ~ New York ~ Toronto ~ Sydney
Auckland ~ Mexico City ~ New Delhi ~ Hong Kong

HB ISBN: 978 1 407116 47 1
PB ISBN: 978 1 407116 45 7

Printed in Singapore.

10 9 8 7 6 5 4 3 2 1